Will and the Tiny Magical Island of Guernsey

Written by Joyce Austin
Illustrated by Georgianna Ritter

First published by Dog Ear Publishing
4010 W. 86th Street, Ste H
Indianapolis, IN 46268
www.dogearpublishing.net

ISBN: 978-1-4575-1818-8

This book is printed on acid-free paper.

This book is a work of fiction. Places, events, and situations in this book are purely
fictional and any resemblance to actual persons, living or dead, is coincidental.

Printed in the United States of America

Tonight, sweet baby, you and I are going to rock for a while before you go to sleep because I have a story to tell you......a story and a secret......

It started one warm August morning when a young man named Will woke very early and peered out the window of his family's stone cottage. He could see over the tops of the fruit trees in his yard all the way to the harbor. Will turned his head and glanced at his younger brother, George, who was still sleeping soundly, unaware that this important day had already begun.

Will quietly moved from his bed and began packing his last few things into his satchel. He hurried downstairs to make himself a cup of tea. He was surprised to find his mother already in the kitchen.

"I didn't mean to wake you, Mum," he said.

"I wanted to make your breakfast for you today," she replied and smiled.

Today was to be a very special day. Today Will was leaving for America.

The year was 1910. Will and his family lived on the tiny island of Guernsey, one of the islands neatly nestled in the English Channel between England and France. Will and his brother, George, had both been born there. Will loved the island with all his heart, especially its clear beaches, winding lanes, and the many sparkling greenhouses where tomatoes and grapes and flowers were grown for the markets.

There were woods filled with bluebells in the spring. There were ancient ruins to dream about and a castle to explore. To Will it was a magical place. But Will's heart also longed to see what was beyond Guernsey's shores and today he would find out. For a young man of only 18 years of age this was to be the beginning of a very brave journey.

After breakfast Will and his family set out for the town harbor in St. Peter Port.

"Pa, can't I carry one of Will's bags?" begged George, who, at 8 years old, thought himself to be quite a strong boy.

"Will, are you sure you packed your warmest coat?" his mother asked for the third time.

When he wasn't looking, she tucked an extra piece of apple cake into Will's bag.

In the harbor lay the ferryboat that would carry Will across the English Channel to Southampton, England where he would board a ship named "Adriatic." He would sail across the Atlantic Ocean for nine days and nights heading for his new life in America.

As Will climbed on board the ferry he looked longingly at his mother and father and his brother, George, waving from the dock. He watched his mother raise a handkerchief and dab at her eyes. He felt a growing excitement as he thought about the adventure he was facing but his heart grew heavy as he wondered, "How long will it be before I see my family and this tiny magical island again?"

The trip across the channel to Southampton, England was uneventful and Will easily found his way to where the Adriatic was docked. He thought it was an amazing vessel. Why it could carry more than 2800 passengers at one time! Will stood a bit taller as he climbed on board the ship feeling very confident that he had made the right decision.

Once out on the ocean the days went quickly. Will talked with other passengers and heard about their plans for a new life on the other side of the Atlantic Ocean. On the morning of August 19th Will awoke to the sound of many feet shuffling on the deck up over his cabin. He jumped from his bunk, quickly tugged on his clothes and climbed to the deck above. Many passengers were standing at the railing, talking excitedly and pointing.

"What is everyone looking at?" he asked someone as he joined the crowd at the railing.

There on the horizon was a statue of a woman, firmly holding a torch up to the sky. It was the Statue of Liberty that Will had read about and she was just as beautiful as he had pictured in his mind. His heart swelled with many emotions. How brave he felt for having made this trip all by himself. How scared he felt of all that faced him. Would he like living here? Would he make new friends and find a job? And would he ever see his tiny magical island again?

After moving off the ship in great lines, the passengers squeezed inside a huge building at a place called Ellis Island, New York.

There, Will had to answer many questions and be examined by a doctor. He had to show documents and certificates, as well as letters from his family, teachers, and employers in Guernsey.

"Who will you be staying with and at what address?" the inspector quizzed him. "And how will you be getting there?" he wanted to know.

"Can you read and write and what do you expect to do for work?" asked the next interviewer as he wrote all Will's answers in a giant ledger book.

"Have you ever had any serious diseases?" inquired the doctor while he examined Will's eyes and ears and mouth.

Will felt he was holding his breath while trying so hard to answer all the questions correctly. He was so afraid someone would say he could not stay and would need to return to the ship.

"You may go now," he was told by the last inspector.

Will let out a huge sigh of relief. Finally it was over.
Now he knew his journey had really begun.

Will boarded a train traveling north to a part of the country called New England. There he stayed in a place called Rhode Island with another family that had moved there from Guernsey. He liked the names of these places. They made him feel at home.

Will settled in quickly. Soon he found a job and he began to make friends. He joined a church where he met a lovely young woman named Alice. But every week, without fail, he wrote a letter to his mother, father, and brother, George, back home. He wrote that his life here was good but he never stopped thinking about his tiny magical island across the ocean.

Quickly the years began to pass. In 1916 he and Alice were married. On a clear crisp October morning the following year Will and Alice's son was born. They named him Ray and as he began to grow, Will told him about Guernsey.

"Ray, have you noticed that our house and the houses of all our neighbors have numbers on the front of them?" Will asked him one day.

"Did you know that on the island houses don't have numbers? Each house has its own name. The house where your Uncle George lives is named Llanberis. It is named for a mountain in Wales. That is why we write that word on the envelope when we send your letters there." Ray found this very curious.

"Tell me more, Pa," he said.

So Will told him about the castle that had been standing at the mouth of the harbor for hundreds of years. He spoke of the stone quarries where many of the men worked cutting great chunks of granite. And he described the dozens and dozens of glass houses where tomatoes and grapes and flowers were grown. When Will talked about the island Ray thought to himself that it must be the most wonderful place on earth.

Ray also learned about his family on the island from the letters that arrived every week. Sometimes something special came just for him. One December an envelope arrived with his name on it and inside was an ornament for his Christmas tree. It was in the shape of a fuzzy black cat and on the back was written, "For Dear little Ray, with best love and good wishes".

It was written in the firm handwriting of his grandmother. He began to wonder more about the tiny magical island that his father spoke of so often and his family that lived there that he had never seen. Ray began to dream of meeting his grandmother some day.

When he turned 18 years old, Ray joined the United States Navy. He was now the same age that his father had been when he had boarded a great ship to come to America. Ray wanted to sail the oceans, too. As Ray's ship pulled away from the dock on his very first voyage he was dreaming of all the faraway places it might take him but all the while he was wondering, "Will my ship ever take me to the tiny magical island of Guernsey?" for that is what he longed to see the most.

Meanwhile the years had passed quickly in Guernsey, too. Will's brother was no longer a little boy. George had grown into a fine young man. He had married and started a family.

"What do you hear from Will this week, Mum?" George said to his mother one day while visiting her on his way home from work.

"Sit down and I'll fix us a cup of tea," she said.

While she put the kettle on to boil and measured out the tea, she reached into her apron pocket for a letter she had found in her mailbox that morning. Every week George listened to his mother read out loud the letters from his brother in America. Today Will's letter told of his son's latest travels around the world in a great Navy ship. There was much pride in his handwritten words as he described Ray's latest adventures.

And then one day the letters could come no more. The tiny island of Guernsey had somehow gotten caught between the powerful fighting nations of a world war. German soldiers came and occupied the island for years while the war raged on. Many, many months went by when letters were not allowed on or off the island. Will did not know whether his family was safe and there was no way for them to let him know.

When the war was finally over and the letters could once again flow, Will got news of something wonderful. Not only did he learn that his family had made it through the most difficult of times but also that George and his wife now had another child, a son, who they named Keith.

Will's son, Ray, had also made it safely through the war and he continued to travel the world in his great Navy ships. One day Ray heard the most amazing news from one of his shipmates. He learned that their next stop would be at a port in Torquay, England. There the ship would be docked for two weeks while repairs were made and supplies were restocked.

Ray immediately went to his commanding officer.

"Sir, may I apply for leave while we are at the next port?" he asked.

"Fill out the proper forms and have them on my desk tomorrow. We will see what we can do," he was told.

When he learned his request had been granted Ray made plans to buy a ticket for the very first airplane flight he could find that would take him to Guernsey. Even though his ships had taken him all over the world this was the trip he had waited for his whole life.

As his plane flew over Guernsey, Ray's eyes were wide with wonder. He looked down on the tiny magical island for the first time. He could see the beaches and the harbors just as his father had described. He could see the dozens of greenhouses where the tomatoes and grapes and flowers were grown. They made the island sparkle like a diamond floating in the English Channel.

When he landed, Ray slowly walked down the steps of the plane. Turning around, he suddenly saw a gentleman with a vaguely familiar face and a broad smile looking right at him! There was a young boy standing next to the man waving right at Ray. It could be none other than his Uncle George and his cousin, Keith! Ray rushed toward them with his hand outstretched. Uncle George put his arm around Ray's shoulder and pulled him close.

The circle was complete.
Will's family was together again on the tiny magical island of Guernsey.

And so, my sweet baby, that is my story. But what is the secret you are wondering?

The secret is that this is a true story. You see, I am Will's granddaughter and you are George's great grandchild. And now 100 years have passed since Will first set foot on the ship that took him to America. I still live in New England and you live on the island of Guernsey. And even though hundreds of miles of ocean still separate us, our family is still a family, and has been through all these years. And that, my sweet baby, is what is most magical after all.

AFTERWORD

Will and the Tiny Magical Island of Guernsey is based on the true story of my family. Ray was my father and Will and Alice were my grandparents. While growing up in Rhode Island I heard my grandfather speak frequently about Guernsey. He read the letters to us that came every week from his family there. I can still remember how they were always written on the most delicate, thin "Air Mail" stationary in an effort to keep the cost of postage down. I remember that anything that came from Guernsey was always handled with a special kind of reverence. I grew up believing Guernsey must be the most special place on earth and we were all so lucky to have family there. My great grandmother, Will's mother, was still alive then and, in fact, she lived to be 103 years old. I remember when she was about to celebrate her 99th birthday. It was such a novelty that my whole grade school class made a card to send to her with the signatures of all the children on it.

Will did return to visit Guernsey 3 or 4 times in his life. When he and Alice traveled there in 1949 they went by ship and stayed on the island for about 8 weeks. My grandfather wrote daily entries in a travel journal that I found years later when I was cleaning out my parents' home. It is an incredible view into life there at that time and it is clear from his writing that time spent with family was important to them all. There are also many references to gardening and greenhouses, and growing fruits, vegetables and flowers. Sometimes the activity of the day would be to go to someone's home to help with a particular task in their garden. In the box that held Will's journal was a list of flower seeds that he was apparently preparing to bring home to New England.

As a child I also heard my father's story of his only trip to Guernsey which occurred at age 35 when he was in the Navy in 1952. He often told the story of his grandmother, Will's mother, who was then in her mid 80's. She was apparently still in very good health and when she took him out walking to show him the island he said he could barely keep up with her!

My first trip to Guernsey was when I was in my early 20's. A friend of mine and I had planned a trip to Europe and I asked if she would mind if we flew to the island for just a day or two. I will never forget flying over the island for the first time because it was just as my father had described it – covered with glass greenhouses that just made it sparkle! My great-uncle George met us at the airport and as soon as I saw him I knew right away who he was. He and his wife, my Aunt Nell, were so kind to us during our visit. Having heard about this magical place and my Guernsey family my whole life I could barely believe I was there. It turned out to be just as wonderful as I had imagined.

One day in 1993 I came home from work and found a message on my answering machine. It was from my father's cousin, Keith, Uncle George's son, whom I had never met. He said he and his wife, Val, were coming to New England and they asked if it would be possible to visit us. I was so excited to meet the next generation of my Guernsey family.

Since then our visits have continued and I have been back to Guernsey to visit Keith and Val several times. The most recent trip was with my husband, son and daughter in the spring of 2011. It was specifically planned to commemorate the 100th anniversary of Will's immigration to America. In spite of the many miles that have separated us, our family has stayed connected through the years. It was my desire to continue passing this story along to our future generations that prompted me to write this book.

Joyce and Keith on the island of Guernsey 2011

CPSIA information can be obtained
at www.ICGtesting.com
Printed in the USA
BVXC01n1542131017
497547BV00001B/2